CHANGING IN TIMES OF CHALLENGE

A 21-Day Devotional for Men

Written By:

Dohn Norwood, II

ISBN: 978-1-7364457-0-9 (Paperback)
978-1-7364457-1-6 (E-book)

Library of Congress Control Number: 2021900474

Front cover image by Prize Publishing House, LLC
Book design by Prize Publishing House, LLC

Printed by Prize Publishing House, LLC
in the United States of America.

First printing edition 2021.

Prize Publishing House
P.O. Box 9856
Chesapeake, VA 23321

www.PrizePublishingHouse.com

TABLE OF CONTENTS

FOREWORD

Continue Steadfastly in Prayer – Colossians 4:2

As I write these lines in a small cottage in Los Angeles, it is the beginning of a new year. There is nothing apparent in its newness; Death is stalking the world in the form of Covid; as of yesterday, one person was dying every ten minutes in Los Angeles County. Our hospitals are overwhelmed, stricken patients are on gurneys in hallways and even gift shops, and they are the "lucky" ones; many ambulances and emergency vehicles are being turned away from hospital doors. My eldest son told me yesterday he received a neighborhood text from L.A.P.D and the L.A. Fire Department encouraging people "to be safe," because if they called 911, chances are, no one will come.

These are dark times, the Enemy is rejoicing, oh how he will twist these events into his own tools of Doubt and Deceit. He whispers into the ears of believers, "So *this* is the fruit of your Savior?" How busy he must be constructing personalized lies for us all.

Just a week ago, we celebrated the birth of our Christ in another dark time, a decree went out the whole empire should be counted and taxed, as recorded in Luke 2. A taxing time, a time of trials and tribulations, not just for the world in general, but for Mary and Joseph in particular. *How could this be?* Joseph must have thought, *my "virgin" wife pregnant?* Not only must he bear this fact that must have triggered ridicule, but he must make an arduous task to a distant city, still loving Mary and taking some succor in her stoicism in her quiet endurance of her swollen condition, which must have been further extremely uncomfortable on the back of a mule.

And surely, they must have had an unspoken dread of Mary nearing her delivery date with no place to give birth. Doors to inns literally closed in their faces. You know the story. Out of the darkness our Savior was born, and I have always loved the angel appearing before the shepherds, proclaiming *great news, great joy*, even in the dark times. The multitudes in the heavens praised and sang *Glory to God in the highest heaven, and peace on earth to people he favors!*

It would be a long time before Jesus could grow into adulthood and walk among us as he did and does today. Yet the Enemy is wise and crafty, but there was nothing he could do to stop Mary's delivery in that stable, the portent of our own delivery into Christ, our ultimate salvation. We only have to call on Him and dwell in Him and pray to Him for our deliverance.

It is cliché to make a list of New Year's Resolutions, yet I again to resolve to enter into my prayer life more earnestly. Ever pick up your book of daily devotions and find the page marker set in the previous week or month? I confess I have, more than once. Do I think I have everything I need and yet not Christ? Let him show me my soul-less poverty. My necessities are so deep I cannot be made whole until I am in Heaven, and I must never forget to keep prayer on my lips and in my heart. I was once told "Whatever God has made prominent in His Word, He intended for it to be conspicuous in our lives."

As I understand it, my good friend Pastor Dohn Norwood intends this book to encourage individuals to study The Word daily and to dwell in it, so that they may exercise His teachings and principles in a practical manner in our lives. May you resolve to do that in the coming year, may this not be a book with a forgotten bookmark. And remember in these dark times, when the

world seems out of control, that that can encourage us to seek a Higher Power, a God who is *in* control. And never forget that

even though our calls to 911 here on earth may go unanswered,
Jesus Christ is one Responder who will always arrive, no matter
what our emergency may be.

God's Peace from Los Angeles, Jan. 1, 2021

Mark Richard

Author, *House of Prayer No. 2*

DIVINE POSITIONING

But I want you to realize that the head of every man is Christ, and the head of the woman is man, and the head of Christ is God. - 1 Corinthians 11:3

INTRODUCTION

Changing In Times Of Challenge

In our Christian walk, we will face many trials, but these trials are not just to test us but to shape and mature us in preparation of a new thing that God is developing in our lives. For this reason, "obedience is better than sacrifice" (1 Samuel 15:22) for it readies us for what is to come which will be even more challenging. This chastening is not only to get us through our current circumstances but to build us into a new person sharpened and crafted for the future. We must see each crisis as an opportunity as Joseph did in the Old Testament (Genesis 37, 39-45). Both our burdens and our blessings teach us lessons and enrich us. For what we sow today, we reap tomorrow (Galatians 6:7-9). Each lesson has within it a holotropic element which moves us toward wholeness and brings us closer to the Christ-like man and woman that God created in His image in the Garden before the fall.

In Genesis, Joseph kept his mind fixed on God and His ways. Seeing opportunity within each crisis he faced, he surrendered to God and stayed obedient to His commands. Joseph remained assured that God has power over all things (Psalms 103:19) and that God's intentions for him must be for the good (Romans 8:28). No matter how many times he was betrayed or let down by various people in his life, Joseph stayed obedient to God's commands and was ultimately blessed to fulfill his destiny of greatness (Genesis 37:2-50:26).

But "how can I do this," you may say. In this modern world we are pulled, swayed, and influenced by a myriad of personal and social issues. We must, as Joseph did, look to God and His character which can be referenced in the Bible. Whether it be

Joseph, Moses, David, Solomon, or any man of greatness referred to in the Word, the journey of their lives fulfilled God's will and built a foundation of wisdom for generations of men to come. In the next 21 days, dedicate your mind and body to the Lord's influence through the Holy Spirit that your soul will bring forth the purpose God has for your life.

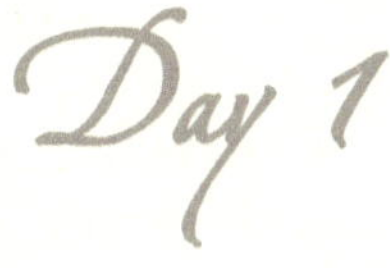

Identify the Challenge

Charge of the Day

Find a quiet place to devote yourself to the Word, a time and space that promotes focus, and begin adding to yourselves as men in today's time of increased challenge. Start and end today in prayer, meditate on the scripture provided, and reflect on the commentary included in this devotional day. In the notes section identify an area in your life where you are currently experiencing challenges to change. Finally, apply this devotion to that challenge and my prayer is that God will move on your situation!

Scripture of the Day

Galatians 5:16 (KJV)

[16] This I say then, Walk in the Spirit, and ye shall not fulfill the lust of the flesh.

Encouragement

Lord, I desire to walk in the spirit in every area of my life. I would like to conquer challenges that are present in my flesh daily. Today's specific challenge has been identified and it is on this day I would like to put it down and pick up Your way of operation in the area identified. I am the head of so many areas and desire to be an example to my family, friends, and community in order to strengthen these institutions. I will practice, today, setting my mind on the ways of the Lord and listen close to the Spirit of the Lord for direction and guidance. I want to stand in my position of leadership as a man and be confident in my ability to carry out my duties. I will tell myself each day that I am a man of God with all the benefits that come with surrendering to the Holy Spirit as a guide. I will walk boldly in the spirit of God and change even in the most challenging times by staying focused on the scripture.

How will I apply this to my personal challenge?

____

____

____

____

Daily Prayer

Lord, today I've identified a specific challenge in my life that I would like to change. I have been reminded today, through the Word, the benefits of walking in the spirit in everything I do. Now, I need supernatural strength from You for the journey of change in this specified area. My flesh is weak, but my will is strong to change for the better. Help me to walk in the spirit in this area of challenge to facilitate change in my life for Your glory and for my good. In Jesus' name, Amen!

Day 2

The Challenge of Change

Charge of the Day

Find a quiet place to devote yourself to the word and time that promotes focus. Start and end today in prayer, meditate on the scripture provided and reflect on the commentary provided during this devotional day. Today we focus on what keeps you from changing in your personal challenge. We will look to scripture for encouragement during this devotional time.

Scripture of the Day

Philippians 4:13 (KJV)

[13] I can do all things through Christ which strengthens me.

Encouragement

We will be faced with many obstacles when engaging in an exercise of change: being overwhelmed by life's daily duties, experiencing tiredness from lack of rest, fighting our first nature as a man, lack of confidence to follow through with how to change, and many other things. The Word tells us that we can rely on Christ as our source of strength. Let us reflect today on the past victories where we summoned and solely relied on the power of the Holy Ghost for a change in a difficult area. Today, let us remind ourselves and recite the scripture in our mind and heart, and say it aloud as often as we can. Let us face the challenge of change with scripture and declaration of God's divine power in our lives.

How will I apply this to my personal challenge?

____

____

____

____

Daily Prayer

Lord, allow me to grow as a believer. Lord, my desire is to please you and to not just know Your Word but to apply Your Word in every situation. Help me to give You two hours and four minutes every day to study and hear from You without distraction. In Jesus' name, Amen!

Prayer for the Change

Charge of the Day

Find a quiet place to devote yourself to the Word and time that promotes focus. Start and end today in prayer, meditate on the scripture provided and reflect on the commentary provided during this devotional day. Today we will focus on prayer specific to the challenge you are desiring to change. You are an overcomer and can benefit from investing in your spiritual health and relationship with the Father.

Scripture of the Day

1 Thessalonians 5:16-28 (NIV)

[16] Rejoice always, [17] pray continually, [18] give thanks in all circumstances; for this is God's will for you in Christ Jesus. [19] Do not quench the Spirit. [20] Do not treat prophecies with contempt [21] but test them all; hold on to what is good, [22] reject every kind of evil. [23] May God himself, the God of peace, sanctify you through and through. May your whole spirit, soul and body be kept blameless at the coming of our Lord Jesus Christ. [24] The one who calls you is faithful, and He will do it.

Encouragement

Prayer is the most important thing we do as disciples and Christians. True prayer involves our heart being open and honest with God and ready to listen and obey (receiving His commands). We must execute and not just be ritualistic. As the head of household and community let us set the example of praying unceasingly (throughout the day), humbly (in His mercy & grace), praising God in advance for what He will do. Give thanks in the midst of the challenge while trying to change for the better. Prayer involves listening as well as talking. Let us activate. Our faith is a relationship (not religion), manage it as we would any dear friendship, while positioning ourselves in prayer. Devote yourself to prayer, be clear, set aside time to talk with God and prioritize time to pray all day today. God wants you in the right place at the right time, that He may bless you. Be in alignment with God and His will for your life. Build intimacy with God today through prayer. Prayer shields us from anxiety and worry, my brother. Allow the word to encourage us as men. Let us allow the Holy Spirit to comfort us and guide us to a place of constant growth and change.

How will I apply this to my personal challenge?

____

____

____

____

Daily Prayer

*Lord, I pray that You allow me to focus on the things that You have called me to manage as a man in this world. If I am called to be a father, order my steps. If **am** called to be a husband, provide me with wisdom. My heart's desire is to be a man that pleases You with my word, thought, and deed. In Jesus' name, Amen!*

Day 4

Anxiety During the Change

Charge of the Day

Today pray at the start and end of each day, devote time to mediate on the scripture of the day and let the encouraging word provided speak to your desire to change in this time of challenge and uncertainty. Specific to this daily devotion is addressing anxiety that may come up when trying to change in a difficult time. Let the Word extinguish your anxiety and the Holy Spirit comfort your worry.

Scripture of the Day

Matthew 6:33-34 (NIV)

33 But seek first his kingdom and his righteousness, and all these things will be given to you as well. 34Therefore do not worry about tomorrow, for tomorrow will worry about itself. Each day has enough trouble of its own.

Encouragement

Changing for the better can bring up issues of self-doubt in our human ability. God is so faithful to not just tell us specifically in His word how to address anxiety but also how we should dismiss our worry about the things of tomorrow. Tomorrow we desire to be better than today but worrying about the process of our change for the better will not aid in healthy change. Looking to the ways of the Lord and desiring to be right with God and

19

following his precepts first will feed the journey to change and worry will be in your rear view. Look to the scripture today. Let it saturate your heart and mind. Tell yourself worry is not helpful to the change.

How will I apply this to my personal challenge?

____

____

____

____

Daily Prayer

Lord, give me a heart to seek Your wisdom first, Your ways of operation first and Your desire for my life. I pray for anxiety to be removed from my heart, mind, and spirit. Remove worry language from my vocabulary. Help me to replace it with scripture and victorious language throughout this entire day. In Jesus' name, Amen!

Frustration During the Challenge

Charge of the Day

Find a quiet place to devote yourself to the Word and time that promotes focus. Start and end today in prayer, meditate on the scripture provided and reflect on the commentary provided during this devotional day. Today we will try to give ourselves permission to be human in our frustrations and allow the Word to help us to extinguish these frustrations as it is not helpful to our change process.

Scripture of the Day

Galatians 6:9 (ESV)

[9] And let us not grow weary of doing good, for in due season we will reap, if we do not give up.

Encouragement

Frustrations usually come from a place of being tired of the exercise of something with little or no results. Sometimes it comes from getting results we do not think are helpful. The scripture is clear as it encourages us in this area of frustration. The Word encourages us to avoid giving up on our situation when faced with challenges. Knowing that each time we face frustration we should initiate a replacement activity (i.e., worship or exercise or even writing our thoughts about the frustration). Let us not let the frustration turn us back to the way we are trying to escape from. Let us meet the frustration with the Word and focus on the reward of change for the better.

How will I apply this to my personal challenge?

____

____

____

____

Daily Prayer

Lord, teach me to discipline my mind, heart, and hands. I want to be a man that walks the road that You have commissioned me to travel. It is important that I model for other young men and whomever You have for me to lead. As I do this, help me to capture my frustrations and cast them at Your feet replacing them with your words of comfort. In Jesus' name, Amen!

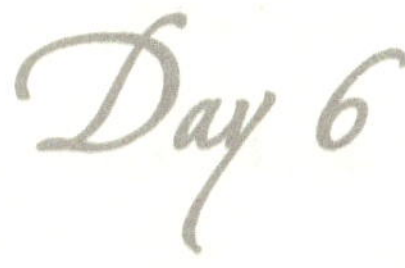

You've Overcome Challenge Before

Charge of the Day

Find a quiet place to devote yourself to the Word and time that promotes focus. Start and end today in prayer, meditate on the scripture provided and reflect on the commentary provided during this devotional day. Today we will offer positive reinforcement to ourselves for winning past challenges and overcoming the toughest changes on our personal journeys. You are doing many things well in life, it's just time to move to the next level of operating as a man of God.

Scripture of the Day

Galatians 6:9 (NIV)

[9] Let us not become wearying doing good, for at the proper time we will reap a harvest if we do not give up.

Encouragement

Listen! You have overcome challenges before this time, and you have seen some extremely challenging times as well and you are still here. That is evidence that you have what it takes to overcome the change in the time of challenge. The Word reminds us that we will get tired, it is human nature to feel worn down by the toils of life. In this season of change, in times of challenge we will remind ourselves of the overcoming power that God gave us through the gift of salvation and knowing that we have some know how from past experiences of overcoming struggles in our past. Let this bring you comfort as you mediate on this day and devote your time and thoughts to the Lord.

How will I apply this to my personal challenge?

____

____

____

____

Daily Prayer

Lord, I pray that today be a day where I recognize my victorious nature. I want to continue to be an overcomer and I know that I have to surrender to Your Word and way in order to conquer those things that may be challenging in my life. In Jesus' name, Amen!

Day 7

Putting on the New Man

Charge of the Day

Find a quiet place to devote yourself to the Word and time that promotes focus. Start and end today in prayer, meditate on the scripture provided and reflect on the commentary provided during this devotional day. Today's devotion will focus on putting on the new man, the man that God calls us to be for our families and communities. We can grow if we surrender the principles of God's Word.

Scripture of the Day

Ephesians 4:21-24 (NKJV)

[21] When you heard about Christ and were taught in him in accordance with the truth that is in Jesus. [22] You were taught, with regard to your former way of life, to put off your old self, which is being corrupted by its deceitful desires; [23] to be made new in the attitude of your minds; [24] and to put on the new self, created to be like God in true righteousness and holiness.

Encouragement

Controlling our thoughts will help us to start the process of change. It is important to track our growth and take on the challenges in order to continue to grow and evolve. I am encouraging you today to take the tips of putting on the new man by learning the Word and what God commands you to do as a man in this world. Then practice it daily and when you fail don't give up. Continue to pray and fast to increase discipline. God always wants us to grow and add to ourselves through the Word and new experiences and offering ourselves as the most excellent example of Christian men.

How will I apply this to my personal challenge?

____

____

____

____

Daily Prayer

Lord, open the windows and doors that will propel me to the next level in life. Lord, give me the wisdom as a man to know the difference between delay and denial. Help me not to get frustrated when I am in a season of delay. Grant me with divine access in the areas I desire most. In Jesus' name, Amen!

A Foundation for Change

Charge of the Day

Find a quiet place to devote yourself to the Word and time that promotes focus. Start and end today in prayer, meditate on the scripture provided and reflect on the commentary provided during this devotional day. Today's devotion will focus on a foundation for change. We can grow if we surrender the principles of God's Word.

Scripture of the Day

Genesis 1:26-27 (KJV)

[26] And God said, Let us make man in our image, after our likeness: and let them have dominion over the fish of the sea, and over the fowl of the air, and over the cattle, and over all the earth, and over every creeping thing that creepeth upon the earth. [27] So God created man in his own image, in the image of God created he him; male and female created he them.

Encouragement

The Christian life is one of service, serving in God's kingdom and bringing others to Christ. Thus, we must live daily as Christians, exemplifying the work God has done in and through our lives which inspires and encourages others to also walk with God. Therefore, we must work vigilantly in putting on our "new man" daily. This serves God's purpose for our lives and His redemption plan for all mankind. Once we are saved, we must put on the new man God intended us to be thus perfecting of the saints in His likeness as in the Garden. There are steps to this transition. The transformation of our mind is the first step. What we think and feel guides our decisions and actions, thus manifesting our lives and our reality. If we seek to change our lives, we must first change our thinking by meditating on the Word and bring our emotions under captivity through the daily exercise of self-discipline or self-control (temperament) to create a new reality in which to live and serve. Therefore brethren, let us put on our mental and spiritual uniforms that we may be readied and equipped to do God's work.

How will I apply this to my personal challenge?

____

____

____

____

Daily Prayer

Lord, help me as a man to forgive those who I feel have offended me. Lord, help others to offer the olive branch of forgiveness as well. Bless my future encounters with others with peace and resolution as you would have me to do as a head of household. In Jesus' name, Amen!

Temptation

Charge of the Day

Find a quiet place to devote yourself to the Word and time that promotes focus. Start and end today in prayer, meditate on the scripture provided and the temptation that will come up as we attempt the act of change in times of challenge. We can grow if we surrender the principles of God's Word.

Scripture of the Day

1 Corinthians 10:13 (NIV)

[13] No temptation has overtaken you except what is common to mankind. And God is faithful; he will not let you be tempted beyond what you can bear. But when you are tempted, he will also provide a way out so that you can endure it.

Encouragement

The adversary knows our weaknesses and what we are most likely tempted by. The power of the Holy Ghost is there to provide a voice of direction and the Word is there to teach us how to flee from the enemy's attempts to tempt us. The joy in this is that God will not allow us to be overtaken by our temptations and is always available to us as an aid as we walk through trying to face our challenges and the changes we are looking to implement in our lives. God is good and loves us. He wants us to win the battle of temptation and wants us to be victorious in the midst of challenges. It is His desire to see us live our best life. It is His desire to see us take advantage of all the benefits He has for us as his sons. Today, take the time to write your most tempting situations and give them to the Lord in prayer. Lay them at His feet and replace them with activities the serve the kingdom building process.

How will I apply this to my personal challenge?

____

____

____

____

Daily Prayer

Lord, you have made me head of the house and a leader with a call to carry out. As I stand through the challenges of the day, whether in the home or out in the world, please help me to remember Your Biblical statues and guidelines. I want to be a man after your own heart. Help me to respond in a new way even to old problems. In Jesus' name, Amen!

Day 10

Peace During the Challenge

Charge of the Day

Find a quiet place to devote yourself to the Word and time that promotes focus. Start and end today in prayer, meditate on the scripture provided and reflect on the commentary provided during this devotional day. Today's devotion will focus on activating peace when dealing with an intense challenge. We can grow if we surrender the principles of God's Word.

Scripture of the Day

Isaiah 26:3 (KJV)

3 Thou wilt keep him in perfect peace, whose mind is stayed on thee: because he trusteth in thee.

Encouragement

God will provide perfect peace to our imperfect and chaotic situation for He is a God of order and excellence. He is an excellent God! The word reminds us that He will offer you an atmosphere of peace as a believer if you want it. God is faithful and His Word is not going to lie to you. If your change process is causing frustration and lack of focus, God is standing by with His arms open ready to offer your rest for your frustrating thoughts and troubled heart. Whether it is coming from being tired of trying to make the change stick or if it is from frustration of dealing with an intense challenge, God has the holding. Trust

Him, know His word, keep your thoughts saturated with His thoughts, and His thoughts come from His Word. Be honest about your current emotion with God and He can offer a solution for your situation. If peace is not close to you, draw closer to God and you will find it.

How will I apply this to my personal challenge?

____

____

____

____

Daily Prayer

Lord, in the midst of challenge please provide peace knowing that You are going to calm the troubled waters and give solutions to our worry. I lay my worry at your feet knowing that You will guide my steps and wash my heart. Lead me as I try to lead in the areas You've given me stewardship over. Grant me with the peace that I need to continue this devotion to a changed behavior. I desire to live in the most excellent way with all who encounter me. In Jesus' name, Amen!

Keeping the Faith During the Challenge

Charge of the Day

Find a quiet place to devote yourself to the Word and time that promotes focus. Start and end today in prayer, meditate on the scripture provided and reflect on the commentary provided during this devotional day. Today's devotion will focus on keeping the faith and our focus. We can grow if we surrender to the principles of God's Word.

Scripture of the Day

Philippians 4:8 (KJV)

[8] Finally, brothers, whatever is true, whatever is noble, whatever is right, whatever is pure, whatever is lovely, whatever is admirable--if anything is excellent or praiseworthy - think about such things.

Encouragement

In the face of all circumstances, we must consciously choose to stand on our faith and the tenets of them. For the adults in faith, there should be enough faith forged within us from various circumstances that as disciples and believers we can draw clear lines of discernment (decision making) and action (behavior). As we stand-fast in the doctrines of our beliefs in moments of challenge, we are aligned with God and His kingdom building. And in being so, we are not only blessed, favored, and protected, we become benefactors to other believers - keeping them empowered and encouraged through His Word and our living example. Thus, we must stay focused as leaders and teachers, as brothers and sisters in the body of Christ. Keeping at the forefront of our minds God's will and purposes, allowing our challenges and changes to be witnessed and to serve as fueling inspiration. God's insight is our sight. Meditating on the Word of God, spending time with God in prayer, and sharing in service with other witnesses will inevitably lead to readily hearing from the Lord and the proper execution of His commands, from faith to faith.

How will I apply this to my personal challenge?

____

____

____

____

Daily Prayer

Lord, Your Word tells us not to be anxious for anything. Please help us to apply this word today and every day. Help us as men to focus on Your thoughts and the things that keep us calm. In Jesus' name, Amen!

Day 12

Rising Gracefully During the Change

Charge of the Day

Find a quiet place to devote yourself to the Word and time that promotes focus. Start and end today in prayer, meditate on the scripture provided and reflect on the commentary provided during this devotional day. Today's devotion will focus on how we can continue to be graceful as we rise from our bad situation into a better way of living for God. We can grow if we surrender to the principles of God's Word.

Scripture of the Day

Proverbs 3:5-7 (KJV)

[5] Trust in the Lord with all thine heart; and lean not unto thine own understanding. 6 In all thy ways acknowledge him, and he shall direct thy paths. [7] Be not wise in thine own eyes: fear the Lord and depart from evil. 8 It shall be health to thy navel, and marrow to thy bones.

Encouragement

God is so good and today we should focus on how He wants the posture of our heart to be as He helps us to rise from the challenge and in the challenge. Now you may feel lion hearted and strong because you are conquering troubles and problems that you may have been dealing with for a long time. This is a sensitive time; we can turn into super judgers and know it alls.

We have to be careful to rise gracefully and with compassion for others, knowing and remembering that there was once a time when we too had the same struggles and remembering that there is always room for relapse. If we continue to acknowledge the divine intervention of the Lord in our change and moment of rise it's less likely we will become proud and boastful. This will be a good shield from relational damages while on the rise. Today practice acknowledging God's involvement in your victorious change and verbalize His power often, every day, and hereafter as you take control of your life.

How will I apply this to my personal challenge?

____

____

____

____

Daily Prayer

Lord, protect me from my own human nature, protect me from a proud heart and boastful speech. Allow me to acknowledge Your presence in my victorious change. Keep me in a mindset of thanksgiving and give me a heart that thirsts after Your wisdom as I rise gracefully from my bad situation. In Jesus' name, Amen!

Using Wisdom Through the Change Process

Charge of the Day

Find a quiet place to devote yourself to the Word and time that promotes focus. Start and end today in prayer, meditate on the scripture provided and reflect on the commentary provided during this devotional day. Today's devotion will focus on how we must continue to seek the wisdom of God for the change and while we walk through the challenge. We can grow if we surrender to the principles of God's Word.

Scripture of the Day

Ephesians 5:15-16 (NIV)

[15] Be very careful, then, how you live—not as unwise but as wise, [16] making the most of every opportunity, because the days are evil.

Encouragement

We have made a commitment to change in times of challenge which can take a great deal of focus and sacrifice. The human side of us is unable to weather the storms that come with trying to make great change within us. The will of a man is weak in its natural state. The wisdom of man is not wisdom at all with the influence of God's Word and the guidance of the Holy Spirit. Today we need to focus on hearing from God's voice and making sure that His knowledge and wisdom is heavily impressed on our hearts. Today we need to stop to reflect on the lack of wisdom we possess and throw away any ill thoughts that we have used to try to change in times past. Today we will use the work and find opportunity to make our days full of change thoughts and change talk. Today we will move in caution as we continue to seek change in the time of challenge.

How will I apply this to my personal challenge?

____

____

____

____

Daily Prayer

Lord, we seek wisdom as we all trust this process of changing in a time of challenge. There are so many distractions and we need Your wisdom to continue to choose wisely as we walk through this time. Please grant us with Your supernatural strength as we invest time into our natural man. Bless our efforts and give the increase to the seeds we are planting into our own change for the better. In Jesus' name, Amen!

Day 14

Instruction for the Change

Charge of the Day

Find a quiet place to devote yourself to the Word and time that promotes focus. Start and end today in prayer, meditate on the scripture provided and reflect on the commentary provided during this devotional day. Today we will focus on what the scriptures say in the area of instruction for our change in challenging times. We can grow if we surrender to the principles of God's Word.

Scripture of the Day

Psalm 32:8-9 (NIV)

[8] I will instruct you and teach you in the way you should go; I will counsel you with my loving eye on you. [9] Do not be like the horse or the mule, which have no understanding but must be controlled by bit and bridle or they will not come to you.

Encouragement

The instruction of God is throughout the scriptures and He is very clear with His instructions, even when we are not willing to accept what He is saying. Let your desire be to gain wisdom through his divine instruction. Open your heart to be teachable in every way. Open your mind to think of the words He has given you through His Holy Spirit. Let the wise counsel of the Lord be your foundation for change. Give way to the precepts and principles that the Lord gives you to carry in your mind and heart daily. Do not be hard hearted or stubborn to the change that will ultimately make you a better man. You are worth the work that will result in a change in thinking and behaving. Ultimately improving your life in every area. Life as a man can be hard, but it is made easier when we live high and walk in a proper position as the head. I encourage you today to walk in your position with confidence that God will give you everything you need to make better choices and be a solid example for your family. Walk gracefully as you seek and find God's instruction for your personal change.

How will I apply this to my personal challenge?

____

____

____

____

Daily Prayer

Lord, help us as men to move with Your specific instruction in our spiritual ears and in our heart. Lord, please allow us to find this instruction in Your word daily and surrender to the Holy Spirit as we are led to build a stronger will for the change to be long lasting. Lord, we are available to Your perfect will and desire to please You in every way. Give us intrusion today as we walk in the steps of Your will for a great change to take place, leaving you with the glory and we will be made better. In Jesus' name, Amen!

Day 15

The Fruits of the Spirit

Charge of the Day

Find a quiet place to devote yourself to the Word and time that promotes focus. Start and end today in prayer, meditate on the scripture provided and reflect on the commentary provided during this devotional day. Today we will look at how the fruits of the spirit can be a great aid in promoting focus while working through the change process.

Scripture of the Day

Galatians 5:22-23 (NIV)

[22] But the fruit of the Spirit is love, joy, peace, forbearance, kindness, goodness, faithfulness, [23] gentleness and self-control.

Encouragement

The fruits of the spirit will remind you how to activate the character of Christ during times of challenge and in times of trying to change for the better. The fruit of love will remind you to love yourself as you work through your own challenging changes. The character of peace will remind you to focus on the divine power of Christ our Lord as His divine power will take away your worry about your own human flaws. Kindness will give you permission to be kind to yourself even when you do not feel worthy of the blessings you will experience after the change. Self-control will encourage you to seek God's Word and the Holy Spirit to guide you as you shake off the old and put on the new. This act of change will require self-control and more importantly discipline.

How will I apply this to my personal challenge?

____

____

____

____

Daily Prayer

Lord, help us as men to exercise the fruits of the spirt as we strive to change in times of challenge. Help us to continue to learn how to surrender to Your character traits as we change for the better from the inside out. Lord, we are available to be used as vessels to model change for brothers who may be watching from near and far and want Your divine power to help us carry out the act of discipline that will foster change. In Jesus' name, Amen!

Day 16

The Blessing in the Challenge

Charge of the Day

Find a quiet place to devote yourself to the Word and time that promotes focus. Start and end today in prayer, meditate on the scripture provided and reflect on the commentary provided during this devotional day. Today's devotion will focus on the blessing after you do the work of changing in times of challenge. It is a great thing to see the manifestation.

Scripture of the Day

Philippians 4:19 (NIV)

[19] And my God will meet all your needs according to the riches in glory in Christ Jesus!

Encouragement

Breaking bad habits that have been dragging you down is a victory for us all. The time you have put into changing in the times of challenge will be helpful for your life in all areas. The blessing of praying through frustration, fasting for discipline, and listening closely to the voice of the Holy Spirit is beneficial to us. The blessing of knowing that you will be a better person for your family, community, and future endeavors is worth praising God for. You have acknowledged the challenges that face you, you have implemented a plan of action for change, and now you can enjoy the fruits of your labor. Relish in the fact that God will bless your natural efforts with His divine power. Blessings come after great burden and you have carried the burden of denying yourself the past 15 days of your natural inclinations. That will turn into a praise soon if you stay the course, this blessing will be evident not just to you but to those who are around you. Find an accountability partner to share your goals with and allow their loving observation to be an added testimony to your change in times of challenge.

How will I apply this to my personal challenge?

____

____

____

____

Daily Prayer

Lord, help us as men to be productive; to not just start a project but to finish strong in all areas. Help us to be focused on what you have instructed us to do and move forward in all areas in life. Help us to produce with integrity and care for others as we rise to the highest level of quality of productivity. Help me to be a blessing to others now that I'm experiencing the blessing of change for the better. In Jesus' name, Amen!

Day 17

The Praise After the Change

Charge of the Day

Find a quiet place to devote yourself to the Word and time that promotes focus. Start and end today in prayer, meditate on the scripture provided and reflect on the commentary provided during this devotional day. Today's devotion will focus on praising after the change. We can grow if we surrender to the principles of God's Word.

Scripture of the Day

Philippians 4:4 (NIV)

[4] Rejoice in the Lord always. I will say it again: Rejoice! [5] Let your gentleness be evident to all. The Lord is near.

1 Thessalonians 5:16-18 (NIV)

[16] Rejoice always, [17] pray continually, [18] give thanks in all circumstances; for this is God's will for you in Christ Jesus.

Encouragement

Praise brings God into the scene. Praise opens the gates of Heaven and the doors of blessings. Praise dissipates worry and dilutes concern and fear. Praise tarnishes sadness and magnifies goodness. Praise and worship puts our focus back on God. It humbles us. It makes the enemy flee. It eliminates worry, complaining, and negative thinking. It makes room for God's blessing over our lives. It invites God's presence. It paves the way for God's power to be displayed; miracles happen. It is important that during this time of praise, after the change, to give thanks always and in all of your circumstances, even in chastening and in His mercy and grace - to be grateful for our growing and shaping in this process. Show gratitude, look to God for purpose and yield to God's will. We must continuously remain aware of the presence of God. We must submit to God's will and His purpose whether we are in good spirts or not. We must declare our dependence upon our Lord. We must build our faith from this great act of change. We must diligently seek God's will despite our circumstances. Praise should be a part of our daily lives. We should not just praise for help or about the victories but even in the failed attempts.

How will I apply this to my personal challenge?

____

____

____

____

Daily Prayer

Lord, I surrender my thoughts and actions to You, and I ask that You allow me to lead my family, friends, and even strangers in a lifestyle of prayer and praise to You today. Let my heart be filled with praise as I carry out the duties of the roles You have commanded me to take on as a man. In Jesus' name, Amen!

Day 18

Meditate on God's Word

Charge of the Day

Find a quiet place to devote yourself to the Word and time that promotes focus. Start and end today in prayer, meditate on the scripture provided and reflect on the commentary provided during this devotional day. Today's devotion will focus on the benefits of meditating on the Word of God. We can grow if we surrender to the principles of God's Word.

Scripture of the Day

Psalms 119:13-16 (NIV)

[13] With my lips I recount all the laws that come from your mouth. [14] I rejoice in following your statutes as one rejoices in great riches. [15] I meditate on your precepts and consider your ways.

[16] I delight in your decrees: I will not neglect your word.

Encouragement

Biblical meditation includes prayerful reflection where you ask the Holy Spirit to illuminate your understanding as Jesus did with the disciples on the Emmaus Road (Luke 24:32). Meditation includes picturing (minds-eye), speaking (saying aloud), feeling (the presences), and studying (the Bible/God's Word, as intended). Meditation is the Holy Spirit using all facets and faculties in man's heart and mind. Fix your spiritual eyes on God's ways and his precepts. Allow quiet time to hear His revelation for your life. Allow His Holy Spirit to order your steps. Take time today to reflect on His character and replace your behavior with his behavior. Use your manual to manage your personality, to make you a living breathing example to those around you. Apply the knowledge of God as you seek His wisdom through your daily mediation. To change in times of challenge you must include the Word to give you instruction and guidance.

How will I apply this to my personal challenge?

____

____

____

____

Daily Prayer

Lord help me to meditate on Your Word today. I want to carry Your Word in my heart, in my thoughts and cry aloud when needed. I want to use the Word as a motivation for change in all areas and circumstances. I want to lean on the Word in my time of weakness and uncertainty. I want to find hope in the Word at all times. In Jesus' name, Amen!

Know God's Purpose

Charge of the Day

Find a quiet place to devote yourself to the Word and time that promotes focus. Start and end today in prayer, meditate on the scripture provided and reflect on the commentary provided during this devotional day. Today's devotion will focus on knowing God's purpose for our lives as men. We can grow if we surrender to the principles of God's Word.

Scripture of the Day

Psalm 57:2 (ESV)

[2] I cry out to God Most High, to God who fulfills his purpose for me.

Psalm 25:4-5 (ESV)

[4] "Make me to know your ways, O Lord; teach me your paths. [5] Lead me in your truth and teach me, for you are the God of my salvation; for you I wait all the day long."

Encouragement

In God we not only find salvation but restitution and renewal. If we take God at His word and obey His commands, we find ourselves achieving every desire of our hearts and His purpose in our lives.

In times of strife and peril, we cry out to God, and in times of blessing and favor we praise His name. However, it is our continuous communication with God that is key. Between the highs and the lows, we must endure, as well as learn so that we meet each instance prepared and readied. In both blessings and burdens, we are to execute wisdom, and in our prayer and praise we are to worship our Lord and Savior. This is the child of God's place with the Lord — being consumed in His glory, manifesting it upon the earth in our journey, and feeding others as we grow. We are commissioned to be extensions of God on earth. His purpose for us is to rule in His place in this realm. We, who are saved, are accountable to the Lord and responsible for our thinking and actions. This is our walk.

Since the fall in Garden, God has set a course back to Him that demands compliance and discipline. Knowing man's nature, God went the extra mile to aid us in our journey by giving us a counselor and comforter in the Holy Spirit that we may move about not in our wits but in His, as well as a book of knowledge and wisdom that may have understanding in our circumstances. In our journey, let us not lean to our own discernment or understanding but the acute insight of God, the creator of all, as we were made in His image and that we may return to our proper place at the right hand of His throne. Walking boldly in God's purpose will give us the confidence and character to change even when times are seemingly most difficult.

How will I apply this to my personal challenge?

____

____

____

____

Daily Prayer

Lord, if I as a man am struggling with choosing to stand for Your perfect will, please strengthen me. I pray that I find joy in Your Word even in times of struggle. Lord, grant me with a heart to carry out Your purpose for my life. Help me to give You all of my disobedience. Help me to seek Your purpose and carry it out in my everyday life, on my jobs and in my community. In Jesus' name, Amen!

Day 20

Walk in Responsibility

Charge of the Day

Find a quiet place to devote yourself to the Word and time that promotes focus. Start and end today in prayer, meditate on the scripture provided and reflect on the commentary provided during this devotional day. Today's devotion will focus on the responsibility in the blessing of change. We can grow if we surrender to the principles of God's Word.

Scripture of the Day

Luke 12:47-48 (KJV)

[47] And that servant, which knew his lord's will, and prepared not himself, neither did according to his will, shall be beaten with many stripes. [48] But he that knew not, and did commit things worthy of stripes, shall be beaten with few stripes. For unto whomsoever much is given, of him shall be much required: and to whom men have committed much, of him they will ask the more.

Ephesians 4:20-24 (KJV)

[20] But ye have not so learned Christ; [21] If so, be that ye have heard him, and have been taught by him, as the truth is in Jesus: [22] That ye put off concerning the former conversation the old man, which is corrupt according to the deceitful lusts; [23] And be

renewed in the spirit of your mind; [24] And that ye put on the new man, which after God is created in righteousness and true holiness.

Encouragement

Being a Christian is a service position. We as men are held to a standard of leadership in our homes and in the community. We must embrace, "transform", and walk anew: in thought, in speech, and in action as brothers of Christ. We must seek to know the Lord deeply and know His will for our lives. Spending time with God daily will help promote a closer more intimate walk with God. Set aside quality time. I liked to say 10% of my day belongs to God (2 hours and 40 minutes) for devotion and mediation on His Word. Practicing the act of non-conformity to the world is a jog and not a sprint. It takes much practice and discipline. This is why I encourage us as men to include a time of fasting and prayer built within each day. Customize it for your healthy and daily schedule. Take the time to learn and hear from the Lord by including quiet moments in natural spaces. Be mindful of the conversations you allow to enter your ear space and the images you allow to enter you eye space. Seek opportunity to practice righteous acts and seek holiness as much as possible. The discipline of the actions will pay off, my brother.

How will I apply this to my personal challenge?

____

____

____

____

Daily Prayer

Lord, help us at the end of this devotional to respond to the things that promote change in our speech, in our behavior, and in our thoughts. Help us, as men, to fill our hearts with things that will promote change and overcome challenges even when its most difficult. Help us not to give up or be frustrated with our flaws and inabilities. Help us as men to keep pressing, pushing, and producing. In Jesus' name, Amen!

Day 21

A Guilt Free Change

Charge of the Day

Find a quiet place to devote yourself to the Word and time that promotes focus. Start and end today in prayer, meditate on the scripture provided and reflect on the commentary provided during this devotional day. Today's devotion will focus on the freedom in the change. We can grow if we surrender to the principles of God's Word.

Scripture of the Day

1 Corinthians 1:8 (NIV)

[8] He will also keep you firm to the end, so that you will be blameless on the day of our Lord Jesus Christ.

Encouragement

God reminds us in His word that He has done it all for us. The change has happened and now it's time to free ourselves from guilt and shame. Even the most challenging spiritual problems will be forgiven and can be changed by the power of the Holy Ghost and the blood has covered us thoroughly. This is the last day of our journey and today we should remind ourselves that we are forgiven, and we are to walk with our heads high knowing that God has given us a gift. Meaning free with no tricks. His blood has saved us and carried us from our terrible behavior. Today we are free and we must declare that God has given us the opportunity to walk blameless and has even given us His sustaining power. He has fortified us and we should use today to reflect on that.

How will I apply this to my personal challenge?

____

____

____

____

Daily Prayer

Lord, help us help us to understand the onus is on us to be good stewards of the victorious battles we overcome. Being careful to show gratitude to You, God and being an example to the world of the great change that you have performed in us. The challenge was not to break us but to build us into the men you wanted us to be. The change was to get Your glory and make us into a usable vessel for kingdom building. The victory was to facilitate a great testimony to share with family and to serve the community. So, grant us with the strength to carry our cross and run our race as you have commanded. In Jesus' name, Amen!

CONCLUSION

Ephesians 4:22-24 (NIV)

[22]You were taught, with regard to your former way of life, to put off your old self, which is being corrupted by its deceitful desires; [23] to be made new in the attitude of your minds; [24] and to put on the new self, created to be like God in true righteousness and holiness.

On the road to Damascus, Saul an Israelite of the tribe of Benjamin who had been raised as a Pharisee and who was a persecutor of the followers of "The Way" (Christians), was confronted by the risen Christ Himself. This riveting and enlightening moment would not only change Saul forever but the course of the world. Saul's transformation into "Paul" was a continuous shaping conducted by God in His sovereignty through Paul's circumstances. Operating in his purpose, Paul would go on to write approximately half of the New Testament and found what would be the body of Christ on earth, the Church.

As we walk in the light of God's purpose, He will fulfill, in us, the building of His Kingdom on earth, as well as transforming fallen human beings into the Christ-like being we were originally meant to be. He has given us a comforter in times of challenge, the Holy Spirt, and an aid in wisdom in times of change, the Bible, God's Holy Word. We must learn, apply, and execute the principles and tenants of Christ's teachings in our lives daily. This inevitably leads to alignment with God's purpose for our lives and the manifestation of a new life and new being.

Do not conform to the pattern of this world but be transformed by the renewing of your mind. Then you will be able to test and approve what God's will is—His good, pleasing, and perfect will - Romans 12:2 (NIV).

As with Paul, once we receive salvation our next step is transformation. This transformation is achieved in following Christ's commands as we face our various trials. Philippians 4:12-13 teaches the believer that we can do all things through Christ which strengthens us. The "which" in this verse refers to the circumstances in which Christ gives us strength (endurance and wisdom). Christ walks with us as we go through our challenges and these challenges change us for the better. So, it is in our darkest times that we grow.

This 21-day devotional can be used and applied repeatedly throughout the year. In addition to daily devotionals, we should add times of fasting to reset our minds, bodies, and spirits (Isaiah 58:3-7), receiving clarity as we work through various crises and overcome personal challenges. Lastly, as you evolve and progress in your circumstances, bring into remembrance the first time God met you on your road to Damascus. How did Christ address you and what did He bring into focus for you to resolve and what mission did He set you on? This will keep you compelled, proactively driven, and aligned with His will like a tuning fork in times of doubt, anxiety, and confusion. May God's anointing, favor, mercy, and grace adorn you.

Be Blessed My Brother!